IMAGES

FELIX *the* CAT *and* OTHER STORIES

ROY MERCHANT

First Printed in United Kingdom in 2021

Published by Relentless Realities Publishing

www.relentless-realities.com

Edited by: Charles Phillips and Christopher Walker

ISBN: 978-1-9168711-1-3

CONTENTS

DEDICATION

I dedicate this book to my wife Sue, who has shared with me this journey for a long time. We have worked together to develop the next generation of positive, ambitious and loving people.

I also dedicate it to my children Adrian, Ainsley, and Sophie and my grandchildren Kyle and Kanicia. They are our life's work, the primary reason we came to this planet.

I also dedicate it to everyone worldwide who are battling COVID-19. Nature will find a way, it always does. Be positive.

TROUBLE AT
MANGER

1

Mary's Story

'I sat on the donkey on my way to Bethlehem and smiled to myself. I was escaping from the shame, rumours and gossip in my town and using the excuse that we all had to get back to our place of birth for registration to leave Galilee.

'Between my Joseph and me, we had decided to run away from the nastiness and find a quiet place back home in Bethlehem to have our first child. I looked across from the donkey and stretched over to rub his hair and hold his hand. He was gentle and strong. He never said much, just let his actions do the talking for him, and I loved him so much.

'The Great Caesar, Augustus or Octavius as he was born, who had taken over after the death of Julius, had brought the

Roman Empire back as the world's most powerful state when he destroyed all of his enemies.

Mark Antony, his onetime friend and latter-day rival and Cleopatra, Brutus and his accomplices who had killed Julius Caesar, had all been, shall we say removed from office, passed away, or had been murdered, and he was still there. Still standing.

'It was strange that such a powerful man was afraid of a little prophecy. The great Jewish prophets Isaiah and Micah had foretold 700 years ago about a Messiah being born about now. Augustus, being a man who left nothing to chance and an almost obsessive belief in fortune-telling, sages, mystics and mysteries, wanted to make sure that this little local Jewish difficulty would not interfere with his big plans for Rome, and he was leaving nothing to chance.

'I was glad in a way to be running away from my little place. I was getting fed up with the stares I was getting from my so-called neighbours and friends and the nudges I saw every time I met another woman, and all they could do was stare at my now developed belly.

'A sensitivity very rare in the men I knew had touched Joseph, my betrothed and devoted husband. He said nothing when I told him I was pregnant and that the baby was going to be the son of God. He said not a word when I followed it up by saying I had not slept with anyone; I just woke up this way. I did not see any magic lights or hear any mysterious sounds. I went to sleep one night, I dreamt I would be pregnant, and six weeks later, I started having these sickness feelings in the mornings.

'He just gazed at me and asked what night I had the dream when I told him. It seemed to resonate with him because he smiled and said he also had a similar vision that night. He never seemed uncertain about anything. If it were the other way around, I would have been surprised, but he never said a word.

'I was lost and confused until I went to see my cousin Elizabeth, who told me that something similar had happened to her and God gave her newborn baby, John, to her. God had told her to protect her precious gift, as someone who followed him would need his help in about thirty years.

'The journey up the mountain to Bethlehem was difficult and I do not know how the poor donkey climbed that 2,500-foot incline, but with the grace of God, it did, and we arrived late at night. By now, I could feel my baby, knocking on my door and wriggling its way down my body and telling me he was ready.

'Now. I know we came from the family of King David, but we were not rich and famous, with lots of servants to take care of all our whims.

'We were not so poor though, that we would have welcomed staying in a stable, but that was the only place we could find in the time we had available before our baby came rushing out. So, we took it.

'Soldiers were everywhere, looking for this Messiah. They had looked six months before when Elizabeth had given birth to John, but some priests had convinced the Romans and Herod that it was too early for the prophecy. This time, however, they were more confident. The God of King David is good, for he sent the Romans mixed messages. They were looking for a king, a saviour. They could not have expected that he would be born in a stable, so they did not look there.

'Our baby came, and there was no pain. He just came out, and he was just the most beautiful child I had ever seen, but I would say that wouldn't I? Some say that he looked a bit like our ancestor King Solomon, who was dark and comely as he used to tell the daughters of Jerusalem. I did not notice that. All I saw was this peaceful child, who from the time he came out had a profound effect on me, and I sensed that all was going to be well.

'The wise men came, in the middle of the night and they looked at him, and they too smiled. And deep inside of me, I knew that all was well with the world.'

2

Joseph's Story

It is now two days after Jesus's birth. It is a Sunday in the year 748 Ab Urbe Condita (AUC).

This calendar is the one being used by the Romans during this period. 001 AUC represents the year they said Rome was founded.

We are in Bethlehem with Jesus, Joseph, and Mary; the shepherds, who are Asher, Zebulun, Justus, Nicodemus, Joseph, Barshabba, and Jose; and the three wise men, Balthasar, Melchior, and Gaspar, or Basanater, Hor and Karsudan, as the Ethiopians knew them. The enormity of the future is sinking into Joseph. He was a quiet man, never made a fuss about anything. Everything about him was relaxed and smooth as the wood he used to plane as a carpenter, and that's the way he liked it, until now.

Joseph always understood thoughts to be part of his inner world, and they had to be managed very well. He knew words were a very important part of thoughts. The building blocks of ideas that change things for the better or the worse.

A person needed to weigh up and consider what your words and your thoughts implied.

You then had to decide which of those myriads of emotions you should send into your external world as actions. For once you had crossed the border and translated your thought into deed, there was just no going back. And not all thought was worth exploring.

Amidst the muted cacophony in the stable, Jesus opened his eyes and the noise ceased. He kept his mouth closed and spoke to Joseph, using only his eyes. The most primordial communication. The way humans communicated before we had voices and could make noise.

Joseph understood everything.

He saw the alternatives that would be given over the coming years and the consequences of them all. It was up to him to decide which actions would keep his family safe.

Joseph came out of the stable as the moon was in mid-sky and sighed. He saw the silver moonlight reflecting off the Dead Sea and tasted the salt as the waves meandered about way below. And he felt alone.

'God had entrusted his only begotten son to me, a carpenter named Joseph,' he thought. He looked up to heaven and said,

'Father, I place into your hands the things I cannot do, the future I cannot control and the events I cannot envisage,' and as he finished, he was sure the moon smiled back at him.

The wise men and the shepherds had also felt Jesus's communication, although they were sure they had heard an angel speaking to Joseph. They, too, knew what had to be done. Jesus was going to be circumcised on the eighth day. They would present him on the fortieth, and the young family would need to get to Cairo in Egypt before the alarm bells started ringing in King Herod and Caesar Augustus's ears. They had to escape from the paranoia of the depressed King Herod the Great and those Roman soldiers.

The Wise Men and the shepherds waved goodbye to Mary and Joseph as they went back to the reality of their own lives, joyful of the things they had seen. Mary and Joseph went from house to house, hiding and keeping quiet whilst they carried out the Lord's instructions.

On the night of the fortieth day, while the Roman soldiers were coming up the very steep hill to Bethlehem to search the houses again, Joseph, Mary and Jesus were sneaking down the other side and on their way to Egypt.

They would not return until they heard that King Herod had died in the year 4BC or 751AUC. Jesus was now three years old and safe at last. His last journey could begin. The family went to live in a place that would come to be known as Nazareth, where he remained almost invisible.

Mary and Joseph had six other children: James, Joseph, Simon, Judas and Jesus's two sisters, and they all grew up quietly in Nazareth. Herod Antipas had by now taken over after the death of his father, Herod the Great, and ruled all over Judea. He would later have John the Baptist beheaded when Salome asked him to, but all that was to come.

In fact, Jesus was hardly heard of again until he was twelve years old in 6AD, or 760 AUC, when he was seen discussing the scriptures in the temple with the scholars.

The Jesus of Nazareth we know was emerging.

He was going to change the world.

Augustus and Herod

AUGUSTUS

'I was fifty-seven years old at the end of the year 748 according to the calendar Ab Urbe condita AUC, or 3755 to 3756 in the calendar of the Hebrews, whose land we were occupying.

'I had done most of the significant things in my life that I was going to be remembered for when news reached me from one outpost in the Levant that a prophecy was going to be fulfilled. Something about a Messiah about to be born who would come to free the Jews.

'At first, I was not worried about it, because in 714 Ab Urbe Condita (AUC), when Herod had come to Rome begging myself and my old ally Mark Antony's help to get rid of Antigonus who had marched in and stolen his crown, we had backed him and crowned him King Of Judea. It meant little to us, but it meant a lot to him. I remember saying to Antony, my ally, that he looked a bit mad, but he would do as he was told. We had little choice anyway, as we had our own troubles trying to steady the ship of Rome, only four years after the death of Julius Caesar and us hunting down the assassins remorselessly.

'I remember exactly where I was when the news of Julius's death came to me and to the day I die, I will never forget the passion I felt as Agrippa, I and Mark, before he became besotted with Cleopatra, created the new Republic.

'I was always hearing about new prophets, messiahs and sages coming up and predicting the end of Rome and although I did not pay them too much mind, I kept flashing back to The Ides Of March and feeling that had Julius been a bit more attentive he might have avoided his own assassination. The only trouble with that eventuality is that I would not have become an emperor.

'I instructed the messenger to get back to Judea and in-struct 'Herod the depressed', as all his subjects called him, to search for this messiah and inform me at once when he was located.

'I was not worried about a messiah from the Levant. We had to get the maps out to see where Bethlehem was. Had a smile to myself, thinking; 'What could come out of that place?'

'Being a cautious ruler, however, I also planned to cover all options by keeping a very close eye on this little area and that madman Herod from now on. He was a tyrant, but he was *my* tyrant.

'Calls himself great! Herod the Great! If he is great, what in Jupiter's name am I?'

HEROD

Herod had been looking for this Messiah ever since his spies in the temples had told him that the priests had been talking about the prophecies of Isaiah and Micah for a long time. The gossip, however, had been getting more insistent since around the year 746 Ab Urbe Condita (AUC).

For the last two years, all he had been hearing about was the Messiah! Now, whilst he was not a very religious man, being king, he realised the temple was a powerful place and had to be taken seriously, or there could be unimaginable consequences.

The power struggle between the Sadducees, modernisers who favoured the Hellenic or Greco-Roman way of looking at the world, and the Pharisees, a traditionalist sect who believed that nothing should change, had been going on for at least 1,400 years, ever since Moses led the Jews out of Egypt. Herod knew that this latest argument was just that the latest argument. There would be more in years to come, about everything under the sun. What he had to do was to manage this one, and whoever came after him would have to deal with what they found at the time. None of them loved him, anyway, he mused.

He had been looking all over the kingdom to find out who or what this Messiah was. Some said he was the chosen one, a new Moses, who would come and lead the Jews out of bondage forever. Others said that he would be the prophet of prophets or the king of kings. Now, Herod was not all that worried about the prophet of prophets, but the king of kings was something else. That meant taking over his kingdom, killing off his legacy, leaving him as a historical nonentity. Funny how Jesus's existence ensured that Herod's name would last forever, instead of fading back into the obscurity whence he came, but that is another story.

One day during the midwinter festival of AUC 748, his sages came to him saying that a new star had settled over the tiny village of Bethlehem and all the Pharisees said that it was the sign that the Messiah had arrived. He sent his best men, the Praetorian Guards, to look for this new king. They went and looked at all the places they thought a king would stay in, or being born in, but could not find him. They reported back that there was no king born in Bethlehem that night.

'The next day, I mean the next day, 26 December, the messenger from Augustus came. He did not even knock, just pushed the guards out of the way and barged into my sleeping chamber, where I was busy entertaining a new wife and demanded that I got dressed and tell him what I knew about the rumours about some Messiah. I wanted to scream. If I heard that name one more time, I was going to kill someone. The look he gave me told me I had better calm down. Therefore, I did.

'I felt humiliated. I, the son of Antipater, the ruler of

Batanea, Peraea, Samaria, Galilee, Judea and Idumea, the one who had made Judea yield to the power of Rome, was being treated as a powerless pawn by a messenger, the messenger, I tell you, of Augustus.

'In any other time, they would have seen me as an outstanding leader. My kingdom was the size of David's at its most powerful. I had made an enemy of all my kindred people to ensure that the relationship with Rome remained intact. I got more tax collected for Rome than anyone else. The Jews hate me and would kill me with no mercy the minute I show any weakness. Despite that, Augustus treats me as just another vassal. A Roman thrall.

'Survival is the greatest instinct known to man. It overcomes humiliation, overrides bravery and courage and leaves you incapable of doing unselfish things, and I was a great survivor.

'My soldiers searched high and low, up and down the hills, in every nook, every cranny, every cave from the shores of the Dead Sea right up the hill to Bethlehem despite that, we could not find him. We heard that Magi's from another country saw him, that the shepherds had also come to worship him, that he was circumcised and was also presented on the fortieth day. Somehow, he always eluded us. My soldiers killed all the first-born children under two years old as a lesson to the Jews. Still, no one offered a name, an abode, a relative, anything that would give us a clue as to the whereabouts of that blessed Messiah. And each day the messenger from Rome took my failure more personally, almost as if he thought I was failing to find this Messiah on purpose.

'I wanted to create a great dynasty. Nothing like Rome, you understand, even I did not have the ego or energy to sustain the power required to build something as huge as Augustus has done with Rome, but I was fed up to the teeth with just being seen as just a satellite of Syria. I had to be at the beck and call of a Governor or Prefect of Rome who did not even stay in Jerusalem, but had to be stationed miles away in Caesarea. That's almost in Syria itself.

'I do not think that Augustus ever cared about finding the Messiah. He just wanted to tease me, to show me up, to remind me of my incompetence. Had to show me that without him in Rome, I could not be trusted to manage a little domain such as this. I could not even find a baby in a tiny village of about 600 people.

'I heard that the Messiah and his family fled the 250 miles to Egypt and although I was embarrassed at being made a fool of, at least he was out of my hair, and the messenger was no longer in my Palace humiliating me.

'It was in my sixty-ninth year, in 751AUC, when I had achieved all I was going to achieve, and the madness and the constant pain and tiredness from my weak blood flow were making me see things in ways even I was questioning when the vision came.

'I was in my sleeping quarters, having just failed to satisfy my tenth wife yet again and just welcoming the quietness of sleep once more when I felt a presence in my chamber. The apparition was like a spirit. Only it seemed almost holy, almost divine, and of power far higher than any I had ever encountered.

I had seen Julius Caesar; I had met Augustus and Mark Antony. I had spoken to Cleopatra on one of my treks into Egypt when Mark Antony was there playing the fool. These people had personal power and a charisma that you knew was more powerful than yours could ever be, but the spirit of Yahweh's son was a source of grace whose power was beyond comprehension.

'In my quiet contemplation with him in the twilight hours, he walked with me, and he "talked" with me, and his "voice" was soft. No "words" came from his mouth, but we spoke at a primordial level through his eyes. This went on for a long time, while we walked in that garden of his village house in Cairo.

'The apparition told me I was forgiven, that Yahweh had decided what was, what is, and what will be, and that I had no choice in the path I took to fulfil the prophecy. I was told that they would always remember me for the bad things I had done, but they would also remember me as the greatest builder in Israel's history. He told me to close my eyes and feel no more pain. I did as I was told, and the arteriosclerosis pain disappeared along with the pain and voices in my head.

'I smiled, my breathing stopped, and I was no more.'

4

John, The Precursor

'Quite how I ended up being known by two names, John
the Baptist and John the Precursor. I will never know, but
that is what happened.

'I remember the first time I saw him was the day we went to visit
them a couple of years after they returned from Egypt and were
back in Nazareth. This was after the death of Herod the Great.
There was a grand celebration in the village for the return of
Mary, Joseph, Jesus, and James, my cousin, who came after Jesus.

'There was more relief than a celebration for the third an-
niversary of the death of the mad King Herod.

'Towards the end of his reign, father told me that Herod got
more paranoid and obsessed with finding the new Messiah and

at one point, he thought it was me. Me, I mean me, the Messiah. I have to laugh when I hear that. I was not a Messiah; I was more of a door opener to the Messiah's mightiness.

'I remember us going into the village and everyone running out of their houses to get to the town square to see who the new people were and Mum telling me it was our cousin Mary and her family we were going to see. That they had run away to Egypt to avoid the mad king's purges five years ago when once again he had been looking for a Messiah. The king would listen to his so-called Wise men and become convinced that the Messiah was born, this time in Nazareth, next time in Bethlehem, another time in Jerusalem. His soldiers were all over Judea looking for the Messiah, but could never find him.

'Mary, Joseph and the children had returned about two or three years earlier, and this was the first time Mum and Dad were going to see them since their return. It was the month of June, and the year was 1BC. I was six years old, and Jesus was about five.

'I was standing at the front of the square, looking at all the people in this bustling village, which was a lot bigger than where we lived in Judah.

'Judah was tiny compared to this big town. In our village, there were more sheep than people. My father was a sheep farmer and local priest, and on some Sabbaths, you could count the number of his congregation on the one hand. That never deterred him, though, and sometimes his most powerful sermons were delivered to an almost empty temple.

'In the three weeks we stayed in Nazareth, I never saw Jesus ruffled. He was obedient all the time, even when his father kept telling him to do many chores. He never grumbled, not even when his father was not there.

'From time to time, we would go down to the stream and swim and catch fish and run along the bank, pretending we were chasing monsters such as Baal from the old religion and had to run to the temple to ask Yahweh to protect us.

'It was funny, looking back, there was this one time when Jesus looked up to the sky and seemed to be very sad, almost as if he knew there was something out there that he was longing for and would not get for a long time. But then I might have been imagining it. He just looked as if he was homesick. Yes, homesick was how he looked. But then I was only six, so what did I know?

'Those three weeks were magical, and I still remember them as if they were yesterday. We did so many things that the twenty-one days seem to fill out and became almost like twenty-one weeks. I got to know Jesus then, as much as any-one would ever get to know him, and as the years went by and the memories faded, the events became almost mythical. Sometimes you had to pinch yourself to recall the realities of those twenty-one days. They were our days. Our paths were never to cross again until the last days.'

5

Am I the Messiah?

'I have always been here, there, and everywhere. I am part of what was, what is, and what will be. I am part of the Holy Trinity, and the Holy Trinity is part of me. We are the ultimate life in this universe. We come, and we go, from one galaxy to the next, ensuring that change is always going on. We are at one and as one with this universe and this universe is at one with us.

'I remember that time on Gaia very well. I had not been there for a while, and it felt good to go back there to have a peep at Adam's children. I was only going to be there for a few seconds, just to have a quick look. That is all I need most times as I know in profound terms what is going on, but I ended up staying for thirty-three Gaia years. This is why.

'There is a continuous stream of thought that goes on as communication between the Holy Trinity. We think therefore it is, you might say. I say we, it is not really, we, as in three separate individuals. I suppose a simple way of describing the relationship is to think of it as three distinct aspects of the same individual. Three different and differing dimensions locked into the exact space and time.

'In the beginning, there was a void where thought was the most potent force. Somehow, we thought, and therefore we became, and we have been here ever since. We separated time from space and used all that energy to bring ourselves into being. The energy that is now in this universe, which guides it, feeds it, causes the changes that it needs to survive, is the remnant from our creation.

'The Good Book says that we created everything in six days and rested on the seventh and in a sense that is roughly the right ratio, although if you wanted to be more precise, one of our days is about two billion of Gaia's years.

'One of the sad things about immortality is that in the end everything comes around and around again and nothing, in the end, is fresh. If you add to that our ability to know what is, what was and what will be, then you begin to have an insight into the predictability of our lives.

'At the start of this journey, there was not a day when we did not know what was going to happen and, in the end, our thoughts started to prevent change (which is the engine that drives the universe) from occurring. So, we had to find ways of not knowing what we knew. We developed ways of not being able to see the next 10,000 Gaia years. This controlled ignorance allowed change to become the engine once again.

'We can be anything we want to be because we created everything there is, so visiting Gaia as a foetus in a virgin was not a big issue. We were going to visit Gaia and then spend a bit of time in the Toliman or Alpha Centauri star system, the one next to Milky Way, while we were in the area.

'Something happened on the way to Gaia. We stopped and looked at Adam's children and were surprised that in the last 8,000 of Gaia's years, they had moved away from the moral path and were reverting to how it had been before the Great Flood. Humanity was degrading itself and falling back into the moral vacuum we had seen in Sodom and Gomorrah. That is the price you pay when you allow free will. Humanity was standing in the abyss once again.

'Within a thought, we knew what needed to be done. We used forgiveness and love to free humanity from sin and reintroduce the moral dimension to the lives of Adam's children. It would take thirty-three Gaia years to get started. We would introduce it in the centre of the most troublesome and challenging part of the world because if we could do it there, we could do it anywhere. We stayed until we realised the plan. Alpha Centauri would have to wait yet again.

'Thirty-three Gaia years is a brief time in the overall span of universal time, and to be honest, although Adam's children, like all life, are important to us, this was a minor event in the overall scheme of universal things.'

FELIX THE CAT

CHAPTER

———∞∞∞———

1

'It was another one of those days. They seemed to follow me wherever I went. I get up early in the morning, and it is my intention to do some positive things. It is my desire to put the odd redeeming, virtuous action or thought into the bank with my God so that when the Pearly Gates beckon, I have a little insurance against going downstairs to hell. It just never happens.

'I am thinking this on the way back to my mother's house after yet another day in the life of 'Felix the Cat', Master Dee Jay, hustler, father and lover. I am on my way home, back from Johnson's house, after pleading with him to give me a bit more time to pay the debt I owe him. I did not think that he knew I was going to Jamaica, so when I told him I would pay him next week, he calmly asked me if I was going to fly back from Jamaica months early to pay him. I have to smile;

I suppose you have to have your eyes and ears open in his line of business.

'He caught me in a lie and let us say he was not very pleased. I left Johnson's shubeen, that seedy little place off the High Road just past the Gas Board, and I am walking slowly to my mother's place. I should be in a hurry, but I cannot find the energy. The spliff and the drinks are making my head spin. I feel delirious.

'Mam did all she could for me, you know, but I was always bad. I used my cleverness as a weapon to make life easier. I pushed all the boundaries. Knowing that I was smarter than most people just enabled me to talk them out of hurting me, especially when I was hurting them. Ah hell, I don't know why I am like that, I just am. It is my way. It defines who I am.

'I shout at two neighbours to mind their own business and leave me alone. I shouldn't swear at them, you know. They have been my mother's friends for a long time. Finally, I am home.

'Mam looked at me as if she was seeing me for the first time and said:' 'It's about time. Where have you been?' She tried to hold me, but I was too far gone to respond. I just grunted out 'Mam' and sat down gently on the chair.

'I was late for everything, it seemed. Too late to see Mathew my son, except for that fleeting glimpse in the car as his mother took him to the nursery, too late to pay Johnson the money I owed him, too late to buy any presents for my Dad in Jamaica, who I have not seen for five years and although I had planned this trip for almost a year, I am now almost too late to get to the Airport.

'Just before I had gone to see Johnson, I had rung Mam to let her know I was on my way and to order a taxi for me for 1:00 p.m. at the house. I am home and exhausted. It is midday, the cab is due in an hour, and I have to finish the packing and check to see if I have everything.

'I know I should wash, put on my travelling clothes and do the last check for the journey, but I am tired, and although my mother is pushing me to get up, I am too tired, and I keep falling down. I have been drinking too much rum, it seems. I am glad to be going to Jamaica, glad to be meeting up with my dad again if only to get some rest and a mental and physical washout. Believe me. I need it.

'I think I will just shut my eyes for a couple of minutes and allow my energy to return. As I am dropping off into that quick sleep, I hear my mother talking. She thinks she is talking to me, but in the end, she must have been talking to herself.'

2

'Well, your bag is packed. I like the way you let me do it for you. You know you had to take the plane, yet you just came in the house, and I have not seen you for three days. Where have you been? Oh, you went to see your son, before flying, how is that pretty little boy of min... a mean yours. Charmaine all right?

'Ah boy, sometimes I regret the time when your father and I broke up, you know. Like everyone, I would like to say it was all his fault. Of course, it wasn't. Your father was too religious for me. His faith choked me, and I was too far removed from morality to accept or even understand what he was saying. In the end, I resented his intellect and his goodness and went out of my way to destroy him and them. I suppose having a two-year-old baby did not help, either.

'I was beautiful those days, you know. My eyes were bright. My body was fit. I was the head-turner of Stoke Newington. There I was, pushing the pram and feeling as if my youth had ended. I am not sure I wanted a husband, never mind a baby at that precise moment in my life. I was trapped in the house, with a husband who worked all day and prayed all night. It was amusing in Jamaica when we had nothing else to do, but not now, not in England, where the world was going at a million miles an hour, and if you blinked, twenty experiences whizzed by.

'Ease up and sit on the chair properly. Why do you keep sliding down like that? It's like you have not slept for weeks. What is the matter with you?

'Your father loved me, you know son, and when I left him, there was no other reason for him to stay and get depressed in England, so he went back to Jamaica and as you know trained as a parson and preaches to his flock as many times a week as he can. Sometimes I wish I could reduce all my needs to something so simple. Still, he looked after you and used to send money to me every couple of months. Of course, it was never enough, but it was the best he could do.

'Too late, I realised I loved your father too late. It was as I saw him going through the departure lounge at Heathrow Airport that it came to me. It was then I realised, just as he was going for good, what I wanted in life. Pride overwhelmed me, and I decided to let him go. Besides, I thought I would talk to him when he got to Jamaica about how I felt.

'Your daddy, however, had other plans. Somewhere between London and Kingston, he became even more focused on fulfilling his religious destiny. Never saw again, the man I loved, you know. I saw your father, I saw the preacher, but I never saw that man who swept me off my feet on those cool nights in Mandeville in our youth.

I never saw the boy who sweet-talked my Mam into allowing him to take me all the way to Kingston to see Prince Buster play live in 1963. He just disappeared into the mass of religious indoctrination that immersed him on his arrival in Jamaica, and I never saw that sweet man again.

'Hold on a minute, son. The phone is ringing. Let me just get it.

'It was your friend. He wanted to know if you had gone yet. I told him you were catching a nap; said he would see you at the airport.

Where was I? What was I going on about? Oh yeah, I was talking about your dad. Your father was sweet, and when he left, I was desolate, even though it was all my fault.

'There I was, a mother with no proper way of looking after you. The only family I had in England was my Aunty Martha, who blamed me for the break-up and thought that I was getting everything I deserved.

'I sat down one day and cried, and as I grieved, the solution came to me, and after a couple of hours of tears, I knew what I had to do. You were going to go to a nursery, and I was going to work. I was going to do every overtime I could get. I was going to live in that hospital and nurse people for eighteen hours a day if I had to. I was also going to get a cleaning job to make sure that all my ends met.

'I decided I would not be another black victim in this country. I had created my mess, and I was going to sort it. And I did. No one can say I did not. When I look at you though, son, I am not sure how well. I look at you, and I see that look of quiet desperation that haunted me that evening when I was coming back from saying goodbye to your father at the airport all those years ago. It was a reality that I was now alone and had no one to turn to.

'I see in your eyes sometimes the resentment that comes from always being the last one to be picked up from nursery and school. Feel the bitterness that comes from years of waiting outside the school gate and the suspense that comes from wondering whether your mother will remember to pick you up.

'I hear in your voice sometimes the venom that comes from feeling that you are not important enough to have two parents, that you cannot be all that loved if only your mother lives with you. I hear and feel all that, and it kills me, and no matter what I do for you, it never seems enough, and I can never do enough for you. My guilt prevents me from being objective. My ability to say no is limited, even though my yes kills you a little each time. I am so sad to see how far you have fallen and how far you are prepared to fall.

'It started so well. From primary school, you displayed an amazing ability for Mathematics, Geography and above all else, Art. You were always so good at the school concerts I managed to go and see. Yes, I know that the lady who picked you up from school saw more of the shows than I did. I have explained that time and time again. Look, I cannot rewind the time to make it better. All I can do is try to make you understand. The alternative was to live in a one-room flat, with no options for the future, and I was not prepared to do that.

'At ten, you won the scholarship, and I was so proud because you never looked back. You just got better and better. I do not know what was driving you, but you were inspired. Ten GCEs and four A levels later, you could have gone to Oxford or Cambridge. You chose Bristol, or did Bristol in some fatalistic way, choose you?

'Why you change so much? Sometimes I can't recognise my little boy, who I tried so hard to raise properly. You would never say boo to a goose, only speak when he was spoken to, and showed respect for his elders. Who is this monster that came back from Bristol, with no manners, no respect, nothing except a first-class degree in Media? What is Media anyway? I give them a sweet, innocent little boy and this society gives me back a scoundrel.

'All that education at Bristol University. World at his feet and all he does is deejay, deejay, all the time. This deejaying is going to get you in trouble one day. It has too many bad boys in it, people who have nowhere else to go, who don't have the patience to survive. You must leave them alone or bad things will happen.

'You want some tea, or you want some bun and cheese and milk? No, me not going to give you no strong drinks so early in the day. You drink too much anyway and as for that ganja you always taking, you think I don't know, you tink I can't smell it on you every time yu come through the door. Your Daddy can't wait to see you. Promise to lay some flowers on my mother's grave in Mandeville, when you get over there for me.

'What time you ordered that taxi for? I think it has arrived. There is a knock at the door, and I am not expecting anyone. Hold on a minute, let me just open the door.'

'Mrs Brown, my name is Detective Long from Stoke Newington Police Station. Is your son Felix in, please?'

'Yes, officer, but he has done nothing. He has been here since last night.'

'Mrs Brown, can we go inside, you are covered in blood, and we know Felix has not been in all day. We have picked up Johnson, the man who shot Felix, and we just want to have a word with Mr Brown. Where is that blood from, Mrs Brown, is it from your son?'

'What Blood are you talk…? Oh my God, where did that come from? Felix, Felix, are you all right, where is all that bloo…'

Felix is slumped over the chair and has been dead for a little while, as far as Detective Long could see.

MISBEHAVIOUR
AND LIES

CHAPTER

—◦◦◦◦—

1

He had always thought of himself as a loner. His mind, his way of thinking, was always on a different level from most people he knew. Not better, not superior, just different.

Given any argument about anything under the sun, he'd always be the one to defend the position that runs counter to the obvious point of view.

It didn't make him very popular at all. Most people saw him as a condescending, sanctimonious know-it-all who should be made to shut up at all costs. He saw that kind of person as closed-minded, lacking imagination or, as he was fond of calling them, status-quo's yes men.

What frustrated him was that many people seemed always to want to keep their thoughts in a loop, they never wanted to work with and expand an idea, as an exercise, to a point just below confusion level, where, if your line of thinking had anything at all going for it, it should still be a logical, defined and reasoned thought process.

Yes, there he was again, having to defend his thoughts against society's first battalion. The evening had been one of those that meander from lack of stimulation to utter boredom; you know those events when the socio-cultural mix is wrong, and as you straighten your clothes to enter you also take out your painted smile and put it on.

The smile was spread right across his face. As he sat there, he hoped no one got past his superficial, polite exterior, and into his brown, unsmiling, clinical, always evaluating eyes.

He was always unsure how clearly his eyes communicated his emotions and, being a firm believer in only ever allowing people to see what he wanted them to see, he felt his eyes were his weak point.

As his mind refocused on the conversation, he thought he heard Dorothy saying:

'Freddie and I are so much in love that he just couldn't do anything without me knowing.'

Freddie sat there, nodding his head in all the right places, saying:

'Well, if you care for anyone as much as I care for you, honey, then you do nothing to hurt them, do you?'

The words formed in his brain, forcing open his mouth, but an involuntary look at his wife reminded him 'that is a load of bullshit', might not be the response to the brandy-flavoured crap these two were expounding. So, he just let it go.

What in God's name were these two doing in my home,

apart from wasting three hours of my precious life? he thought as he sipped the fourth glass of brandy in an hour.

He didn't know Freddie or Dorothy. They were remnants from a now-defunct dance class, his wife had dragged him to in one of his rare moments of weakness.

His wife was one of nature's rare creatures. She fitted the stereotype description. She lived on a superficial level, saw nothing but good in everyone, was flighty, whimsical, and went through other people's bubbles as if psycho-protective zones did not exist. As a result, she gathered friends like magnets gather iron filings.

That is how we got friendly with Freddie and Dorothy. He thought. A few weeks before, they'd been invited to dinner by Dorothy.

The next week, of course, it had been our turn. We then got invited back, and now it was our turn again.

Now, the first week we exhausted any fundamental similarities between us, the next week was for any differences, so two gatherings later, all we had left were the smiles and the inane, banal comments that were coming out.

CHAPTER

2

The exact date the affair started, the reasons and the intensity of the affair were things he did not know. However, he knew Freddie and his wife were having an affair.

The signs were there. He had not done so many observations and experiments on body language, not to pick up the very loud signals Freddie was giving his wife, although that wasn't the conclusive proof.

The proof was coming from his wife who, not realising Freddie's very low sensitivity, was using a subtle narrowing of the eyelids to warn him that her husband had sensed something was out of place. She then looked at her husband to check whether he had seen her, but she was too slow. By then, his mind and eyes had moved to abstract thoughts, leaving her convinced that he'd seen nothing.

Freddie misread what she was thinking, took it to mean a promise of things to come, rather than a warning. He smiled with his eyes. Dorothy, with her incessant rambling, missed the playlet.

He looked at Freddie and became disappointed with his wife's choice of a lover.

Dorothy's husband was thirty-five or thirty-six, balding at the front and would look much better in contact lenses, rather than the John Lennon- type spectacles he wore.

Freddie grew up in the sixties when one put on the first thing that jumped out of the wardrobe. His bright flowered shirt did not go with his red stovepipe jeans, blue socks and sandals.

If Freddie, in all his glory, got to her point, then anyone else could. The thought filled him with remorse, as his mind's eye started the queue of likely prospects and made it longer and longer and longer.

How could she? Why would she? Want another man. Has she always wanted, no, had other men? Why had he not picked up on this before? He was now becoming apprehensive.

He sat back in the armchair he always seemed to be in on these occasions, held the brandy in both hands and used it to cover his eyes whilst at the same time he took a large gulp and waited.

It took about fifteen seconds for that glow to reach the pit of his stomach, another five to massage and ease the tension that was building up in his head. Then he coldly turned and looked at his wife.

She was still beautiful, always had been. There hadn't been a moment in the fifteen years he'd known her when he hadn't thought that.

She was thirty-four, passing for twenty-six. Tall, pouting lips that didn't need lipstick, a light coffee complexion, with long bouncy hair that had seen every black culture style since cold perm was invented.

Her eyes were the most innocent eyes that ever graced a woman. They were dark brown and warm. Always warm. Her skin was as smooth as ripple-less silk, and he was getting aroused just thinking about her. Yet he knew she was unfaithful.

'Infidelity, that word just never came up about our relationship before. I mean, where did she get the time? We worked together every day in our business. She rarely ever went out on her own, always wanted to drag me with her, where ever she went, and yet!

Well, ever since my business trip to the States, her lips have been cold. I thought I imagined it, but thinking about it now, that luscious peach-like taste and feel of her mouth, that, that warm pouting of her lips had been replaced by a cold, hard faraway feeling, as if she was tense, but no, she is **never** anxious with me, and yet!

The caress, when I got off that plane, was not a lover's hug. Not a fifteen years lovers' caress.

Her body was like an actress, trying to remember her lines, her position, her composure, ten seconds before the most significant scene in a film.

I don't have any clear, hard evidence to say she is having an affair, no physical evidence. Just my feelings and knowing her, the way I do. It is just my imagination, and yet!

Why hadn't I thought of anything like this before? I mean, with her personality, I would have done, if I was the overprotective type.

Oh, thinking about it some more, there is also the love-making my first night back from America. She always used to make love with her eyes closed and her mouth open, her tongue doing circular moistening movements on her lips. Her nostrils would be flared, with her breathing following the slow, undulating motion of our bodies.

That night we lost rhythm five times. Her eyes were opened and her mouth clenched. When I asked her about the tears, she said she was just glad to see me home safely.'

'Darling, darling, you're not dozing in front of our guests, again are you?'

The voice was phoney-sweet, with a hint of edginess creeping into it. It was his wife, dragging him from the labyrinth of his mind and back into the little dinner party.

Freddie got up at that point and said:

'Come on, Dot, I think we're keeping these two old fogies up.'

His wife, in almost a pleading voice, with eyes locked into Freddie's, said:

'No! Don't go just yet. It's only 10:15. You know him, once he's in that armchair with a drink in his hand, that's him for the night.'

The voice was mocking. The one she used on people she hated. And that jolted him back to reality. She had never spoken about him like that before, at least not to his face.

'Was that how she talked about me to Freddie? Mockingly!'

'She was ridiculing, hating, yes, almost hating. I did not want to say that but yes, hating. The affair was much deeper than I thought.

Obviously, it must have started when I was in the States, or maybe it had been maturing for a long time and the fruit, being ripe, was consumed while I was away for those two weeks.

Let's see. We met them two months ago at that dance class, then a week later I had to go to America, then I came back and a week after that this round of endless nights in our house and Freddie's.

Does Dorothy suspect anything? No, I don't think so. She has spent no time at all seeing anything but the superficial layers of life, so to her, there is nothing else. She wouldn't, in fact, couldn't, suspect.

I am going to leave this until an opportune moment, but I must talk to her about it, he thought.'

They stood at the doorway, waving Dorothy and Freddie goodnight. After three attempts, Freddie finally got the car started and drove off, with Dorothy still rambling incessantly.

They came back to the lounge and sat down, both sighing with relief for their own different reasons.

'Do you want a drink?' he said. 'Martini or brandy? he kept on before she could reply.

'Brandy, please,' she said with a laid-back smile. She then fell back in the lounge chair and stretched. The look she gave him made him feel guilty and apprehensive, for some strange reason.

'Why the look?' he asked, trying to think of a way of controlling the conversation and extracting the information he was seeking.

'Oh nothing,' she lied, even so, she was looking for a sign, a clue, anything that would give her the information she was seeking.

'Who is it and is it over, darling?'

The words froze his thoughts, made him convulse. The drink went down his gullet the wrong way, and he choked.

She hit him on the back to stop the coughing, gave him some water to drink, and waited.

'What do you mean, what are you…? What are you talking about?'

he said after he had recovered.

'You're the one who is having an affair, love, not me. Or is Freddie my imagination?'

'Partly, darling, yes. I gave Freddie the come on, but I made sure that Dorothy could not see it. I have never in fifteen years looked at another man with serious thought.'

She stopped talking, sipped the brandy, then continued:

'Remember earlier on tonight, how you felt when you thought I was having an affair, well, I've felt that way since you came back from America.

'That first kiss at the airport made me freeze. You were icy, and you are never cold. You tried to choke me with your tongue, and you always kissed so gently, like the melting of marshmallows.

'I told you fifteen years ago that I hated you for pushing your tongue halfway down my throat. There you were doing it for the first time since that day.

She stroked away a tear with the back of her wrist, took another sip, gathered her dignity and poise, shook her head and carried on.

'You held me in your arms, or should I say, you held someone in your arms because it wasn't me you were holding. Normally, you hold me with your left hand and stroke my back up and down and my God there you were holding my buttocks in public. As for that first night back when we made love, well, I just felt as if a total stranger was raping me. You weren't making love to me. Felt like I was being screwed like some tart. We were not making love.

'There was no foreplay, hammering away like a bloody dog, and then had the cheek to ask me what was wrong.

'Are you so insensitive to think that I wouldn't know? I have spent most of my life loving the very air you breathe, yet you didn't think I would know that you had been unfaithful. Just bloody remember this, you sod, that was your first and last shot. The next time, I **will** just leave.'

He sat there not saying a word, not even breathing, just thinking;

'She knew, she knew it all the time.'

CLIFTONVILLE

CHAPTER

1

Vladimir stood there looking down into the gorge and was becoming transfixed by the fear that was manifesting as cold sweat on his face, under his armpits, and on his chest. Yes, he had been here before. Now he was going to put the Clifton suspension bridge to rest.

From the first time he'd laid eyes on it, all those years ago, he had known that he was afraid of heights. He had vowed not to allow things such as fear to stop him from achieving what he wanted. He decided nothing would keep him frozen, keep his wings stapled to the branch and prevent him from flying.

So, he came back now to walk across the bridge. To stop in the middle and peer over the ledge and allow the nausea to sweep over and through him. To allow the haunting voice in his head to keep saying, keep going, keep going as he bent lower and lower and allow the 250 feet to the bottom of the gorge, to beckon and entice him, to keep going.

He first came to Bristol in 1984, when he was eighteen and had just come over from Paris. He'd been living in that most beautiful of cities since his parents escaped the USSR and its communist regime. Now in 1984, he came to Bristol to study at the University.

His course was Political Science, and he was attending lectures at the School for Advanced Urban Studies college or SAUS, as they called it in Clifton. The school's lecture rooms are a stone's throw from the bridge. As Vladimir sat there staring out into space that first morning, he saw the outline of the top of the bridge looming as though it was living in space and had no contact with the ground.

At lunchtime, he and Patricia, another student on the course, struck up a conversation, out of which came the idea to look at the bridge after the Bakewell tart and custard dessert. Well, you couldn't keep Patricia away. She was fearless. She jumped on top of the guardrail and spread her arms as if she was going to fly off the bridge and be free. Vladimir, meanwhile, was trying to smile, as nausea welled up in his stomach and made itself clear on his face.

This was the first time he'd focused on the fact that he can't stand heights and although he was having an interest in Patricia, he could not hide his fear. And she could not return the attraction. She was a "liver", someone who lived life to the full, who was always going to push the boundaries of her seventy years on planet Earth and had no time for anyone who could not do the same.

He strolled back into class, and he could feel the light dimming from her curiosity with each step they took back from the bridge into the classroom. They never spoke to each other again.

Vladimir went back to the bridge the next day, if only to see if yesterday was a mistake, a happenstance, something that occurred when his courage wasn't looking. His father had always told him to stare his fear in the face and keep on staring until the fear gave up and ran away. So, this time, he asked Walter to go with him.

Walter had fears that Vladimir had not even heard of, and one look at the bridge and its ominous profile gave him a level of foreboding that he had never experienced before. He scuttled back in an almost apoplectic state to the University, with Vladimir holding his arm, to make sure he crossed the road, safely. "Thanks for nothing." Vladimir thought.

He felt that the bridge had something ominous about it and thought he would leave it alone for a few days, despite what his father had drummed into him. He decided to ignore it for a few days and do something at the weekend when there was more time; he felt at ease with himself. At least it was going to happen, and he could look his father in the eyes. Well, partly anyway.

Johan was a troubled soul. He always had been. He, too, was on the Political Science course and had secretly been going up to the bridge in the middle of the night and peering over into the nothingness that he saw below him. Strange, he thought, the longer I look, the closer the riverbed seems to be. Even though it is 250 feet below, the louder the voices beckoning me seem to sound and the more enticing is the whole idea of just letting myself go to see the outcome.

So many miles away from his Austrian home, no confidence in his English and feeling that the course he was on was only to fulfil his father's dream, to maintain his lineage, his familial duty. All he ever wanted to do was paint, but no one in the family recognised that. No one saw the talent that he had. In the Art classes of Vienna, he was developing a strong reputation for landscapes.

Still, his mother, father, brothers and sisters told him he was wasting his time and should concentrate on learning things that would ensure that the family was still dominant in fifty years. That was his duty, not wasting time getting his hands dirty with paint. He would never be Leonardo da Vinci, and there was no point in being a mediocre painter.

On the Thursday night, he had been to the pub and had sat in the garden looking down into the gorge, as the river Avon meandered its way across Somerset. At closing time, when everyone else turned right to walk back to the halls, he quietly turned left and walked to the bridge. He walked to the middle of the bridge, climbed onto the railings, bent forward, and gravity did the rest.

Vladimir never went back onto the bridge in 1984. After Johan's death by suicide, the police closed the bridge while they searched the area for his remains. He did not fall cleanly into the river. The wind had dragged him onto the rock face, and it smashed him to pieces. His remains, or the bits they could find, went back to Austria after the post mortem.

Although Vladimir was at Bristol University until 1987, he just could not find the strength to go back to Clifton and stayed in the halls in the centre of town. In June 1987 he left Bristol, but always knew he would return. There was unfinished business.

Isabel looked at Vladimir and smiled in a puzzling way to herself. Married since 1990, some twenty-five years ago, in that little church in Montmartre. Three children, working all over the world for the United Nations. Been to London at least ten times and he never mentioned wanting to come to Bristol, where he went to University, never mind Clifton.

Why were we going there? Was it some unfinished affair he wanted to put to bed, some place he wanted to see for the last time? He had not said a word about where we were going all the way down from London. All he said was that he just wants to finish something.

He came out of the taxi, paid the fare, took Isabel's arm and started walking up to the bridge. It had changed. There were now security rails everywhere, and you could not just walk up and climb onto the railings. Vladimir walked slowly to the centre of the bridge, stayed on the pedestrian walkway, and peered over. Then he explained what had happened back in 1984 and how he had to come back to control his fear.

Vladimir stood up, grabbed the railings and looked over the bridge, down, down into the gorge and heard the wind whistling into his ears and it sounded like the Sirens whispering to him, that the water was lovely and he should come and join them. He peered even closer when he felt the love enveloping him from Isabel as she put her hand through his arm and gently massage his back. And no longer afraid, the Sirens just disappeared.

A LITTLE TALK
WITH ROCHELLE

'I sat there with my elbows on the table drinking a cup of tea. My mind wondering how I was going to break the news about how it all felt to me about my relationship with you, my daughter.

'You are my last child. You're now twenty-six years old and I have been absent for about twenty of those years. It was not a physical absence, you understand, I mean I was there in body, the physical me was always there, my wife would say, perhaps too much, impeding your crowded lives.

'My emotional, mental, soulful life, though, has been absent, peering through the dark mirror of time at you growing up. Preoccupied with my passion to stay alive, to keep going for one more day.

'It felt like life had decided not to give me a future in Elysium, only the sunless alternative called survival. I kept looking at the school photographs as each year they reminded me of another season missed, another opportunity gone to be her dad. An entire childhood littered with fear instead of courage, hopelessness instead of hope, anxiety instead of joy.

'You were six years old when I left on a late Sunday evening after the chicken, rice and peas, and beetroot juice. All of us were getting ready to watch 'Jungle 2 Jungle' (our favourite film) yet again.

'I was fifty-one years old, Patrick Oliver Thompson, and when I came home again six weeks later, I had changed to Patrick Thompson. I left Oliver on the bed where his heart stopped and the operating tables where they put the mechanical controller in my heart. And you were never to see that me, your old Dad, again.

'Never again see that fearless, carefree, anxiety-free smile, that laughing face whose eyes shone full of confidence in a bright future. And you can't remember who Patrick Oliver Thompson was, what he looked like, how gentle he was. How much love he showed rather than just felt. And I owe it to you to tell you who I was and the life I would have shared with you if I could have chosen Elysium instead of just survival.

'Your brothers are older than you. They, like you, have no sense of who I would have become had one of the alternative universes unfolded. They have, however, have seen much more of me than your six-year-old eyes can have known.

'At seven, when the long days of summer holidays came, we would be free to roam and wander across spaces and through timeless activities, I would have carried you on my shoulders when you tired. On hot August evenings, I would swing you around my waist until you become dizzy from the whirl and telling you frightening monster stories under the moon in foreign lands.

'At eight, nine and ten, I imagined I would carry you on my back through forest dales smelling of ripened wild fruits and trees full of leaves that they could not hold on to anymore. The trees would shed those leaves with no hint of sentimentality so that the next year's crop would have enough food and minerals to propel life forward for another year.

'I would pretend I was racing you in the fifty metres race and letting you win for fun, so you could know the joy of winning. We would go for long walks and talks all over southern England, sharing time and space and getting to understand each other, our moods, our whims, our dreams, our likes, our fears, and who we wanted to be as we got older.

'At eleven, we could have spent June and July mornings over breakfast. We would be talking about what we think your secondary school is going to be like and double-checking who you knew would be going up from your old school. After that, we would start dreaming about the new friends you will meet and how you will get to be their friends. I could have learnt to become your friend instead of just your dad. Sometimes I became an old, moody dad, who had other things to worry about, like where his next breath was coming from.

'At thirteen I would have had conversations with you about me. Who I thought I was and what it is like to be a man so that you understand who men are, why we think the way we do, and that we are not the enemy.

'And I am so, so sorry I could do none of that. But Patrick Thompson did his best.

- Patrick tried to show you courage, by how he adapted when adversity showed him no mercy and just kept on teaching him new things about life.

- Drove you all the way to Bath and Bristol and returned you back home, despite his uncertainties about whether his body could last the journey.

- Made sure you went to drama classes and waited outside while his heart was running like an aeroplane engine.

- We made those long drives to school every morning when all he had was anger and resilience to keep him going because of lack of sleep and shortness of breath.

- Moved you into Uni and every flat until he could not do it anymore. That last one in South London really tested him.

- Was still your taxi even after you passed your test.

- Used to bite his lip when you were drunk. And that skirt was a belt rather than a dress.

- He faded to the back in the lean years when he was no longer needed. Dad found that hard, by the way.

- Patrick Oliver Thompson would have loved you to bits. He would have made you proud. But Patrick Thompson did all he could to live and walk in Oliver's shoes and he loves you to the bone.

'And the sun shines, the rivers flow, the trees dance in the breeze. A car beeps its horn in the road. A daughter begs her dad for another ice cream. Father says no. She gives Mum one of her pleading eyes, and mum wilts, gets the Magnum ice cream and continues talking to her mother-in-law, missing the power play. The child looks at her Dad, pokes her tongue out in a smile of victory. Father smiles an ironic smile of defeat, ruffles her hair.

And all is well.'

LIFE AND DEATH

———— ∞∞ ————

1

Life

'I stood there, watching my uncle die. Life fighting for its life. The morphine would try to fool his life into thinking that all was well, but you could see that life knew that its strength was ebbing away and death was getting stronger by the minute. Soon, the curtains would close, the light would fade, and the void would welcome my uncle back into the world of spirits and pure light.

'In the three years that uncle had allowed cancer to go unchecked, unpunished and unmanaged, it had become strong. It had matured to a level where it now refused to die. It was now almost the dominant life force in his body. Like all energies, from obsessions and madness to a tiny seedling, it needs to create its own life cycle, even if that means ending yours.

'Along the way, cancer had befriended jaundice, groomed it into being an ally. Between them they had almost destroyed his immune system, so by the time Uncle realised what was going on, it was all too late.

'When Uncle came back to England from Jamaica and visited the doctors, they looked at him, looked at each other in silence, shook their head and walked away, prescribing painkillers and knowing it was just too late.

'We all sat or stood around his bed, too many of us for the small space, and unwittingly annoying the other patients so late into the night.

'We were all there, putting every ounce of our energies into begging him to fight and not give in. To lock the door and refuse to let death in. Uncle could not let us know whether he heard or even understood us, but I suspect that knowing him, deep down, he would have smiled at how little we knew. For by now he was 'journeying'. His travel back to the long side of eternity had begun, and he must have known that we were still trying to cling onto something that could never be.

'His son looked at his beloved dad and cried, trying to figure out what was in the best interest of the most significant man there has ever been in his life. At last, he knew. Uncle's son could not see his father in so much pain and ask him to stay here for another second, to cry out another primordial grunt as the agony gripped him once again. He had to let him be free of pain. His son cried and smiled and Uncle understood.

'Six thousand miles away, Uncle's other son felt a tremor, a dark cloud gathering in his universe. It only lasted a second, but he knew what had happened.

'Uncle found himself deep within the depths of his own soul, where hope and peace live. He went over to greet them both, and they welcomed him. He smiled to himself, exhaled all the earthly air left in his body and was at last at peace.

'Uncle died at 7:00 am on the Monday in the hospital ward out in the countryside of a distant land he had grown to love.'

2

Death

Meanwhile, in 'The Lounge Of Hope' all his ancestors were gathering to meet him. They had created the 'Lounge' the place of transition between this world and the next, right on the raft stand by the riverbank of the Rio Grande River at Berridale, in Portland, Jamaica, where the mighty river is at its calmest. It was 7:00 am on that Monday morning, the sun was getting into its stride, preparing for the day ahead.

Uncle Dudley was the first to appear, dressed in the colours of the Akan, Ashanti, Maroons, and all the ancestors who lived before the Maafa, the Atlantic slave trade. This was when Anansi the spider god ruled and told great tales of our people of the past and those to come.

Dudley was the boatman, and he steered the gigantic raft to the side of the river and waited. Charleston smiled and spoke to Nag and Sadie. Sadie pushed Mama in the ribs and squeezed Lynn and their mum, Nellie's hand. Nellie whispered something into her husband Jeb's ear, then laughed with her mother Teachie as they all eagerly waited for the new arrival.

Teachie went over to her mum, who was born into slavery, and said something to her. She nodded her head as if she understood who they were all waiting for. Teachie's father, the white man from Scotland, turned his head and looked back into infinity at all the ancestors who greeted the new arrival.

Then Uncle materialised, and as the hospital robe he was wearing changed itself into the Akan colours full-length gown, he smiled. It was a smile of joy, a smile of homecoming.

Dudley welcomed him onto the raft, and all his siblings hugged him until he sat down. He then pecked his mother, Nellie, on the cheek, hugged Jeb, his father, who had died when he was so young, and his grandmother Teachie. She introduced him to all who died before he became human. When the introductions were complete, Dudley took the big oar and pushed it into the silt, clay and sand at the bottom of the river, and the raft moved off.

There was feasting, dancing and merriment as the raft went past all the landmarks until St. Margaret's Bay appeared. The boat kept going until the horizon of the Caribbean Sea came and went. The raft got smaller and smaller until it disappeared from view and was no more.

And you know, although we miss him, Uncle is in a wonderful home.

AN AFTERNOON
WITH MY SON

It was a cold October evening. The previous Fridays had been nice and warm. It seemed as if the last days of the Indian summer were going, and the grass would not need mowing again for another six months.

My son, ten years old and preferring badminton to football, was also a good defender in the school team. A big boy, with a good football brain, he would always intercept and get the ball up to the midfield players, he seldom went upfield himself, preferring to ensure that no one got past him to threaten the goalkeeper.

On this Friday, all the parents arrived early to see how our team would fare against St. Dominic's, the local league leaders. There was a little frisson between the two teams. As well as the best football team, they also had the best academic results of primary schools in West Essex. In fact, they were a beacon primary school, according to OFSTED.

They delayed the match while Reece finished his detention. Mr Witherspoon had tried in vain to get Mrs Jackson to postpone it until next week. Mrs Jackson, not interested in football, took great delight in reminding Mr Witherspoon that next week was half term, and the only thing she would detain was her cat. Mr Witherspoon, kicking himself for the mistake, did a quick exit back to the football pitch, where he felt safe. He had never liked that blessed woman, anyway.

The match kicked off, and they were slaughtering us. By halftime, our team was lucky only to be losing 3-0. My son was our best player.

St. Dominic's score would have been double had he not saved four shots from going in. Mr Witherspoon started discussing match tactics before they came off the pitch.

Our team came out with new confidence in the second half and treated their opponents with the contempt we had suffered. We were all over them, and I was hoarse from shouting, especially when it got to 3-3, and only five minutes remained. St. Dominic's, like most arrogant people, knew only how to win. They did not know how to dig in and fight, so when the pressure came, they fought amongst themselves.

'I was thinking this when from the corner of my eye; I noticed my son with the ball on his left foot going upfield. He went past their attackers and midfielders with ease, dummied their giant lumbering defender, and slid the ball past the goalkeeper, into the back of their net.

'I shouted. I screamed and after the whistle, gave him the biggest hug ever. He smiled and said he did not know what all the fuss was about.

'I smiled. I could see how good it made him feel. It was the best day of his life so far.'

'IS THERE A PROBLEM?'

400 Word Flash Fiction

'Is there a problem?' She asked, looking at me from the corners of tired eyes that had seen too many incidences like mine unfolding in front of her, to get excited.

'Arms folded, she waited for some kind of response from me while I wound down the window.

'I mean, she obviously must have known there was a problem. Otherwise, I would not have been sitting here in the freezing cold for so long waiting for the AA to come and get the car moving again.

'I mean, annoyed is not the word that my vocabulary is picking out right now. This is a new £150,000 car, with only 1,000 miles on the clock. My new car is not supposed to break down. It is supposed to just take me where I want. Then wait until I need to go to my next jaunt or shop.

'Sorting out cars is not something I need to worry my head

about. I get in; I push the start button; it starts. I stop when necessary. I get out, flick the remote alarm button on my way to the shop behind my back, put the key fob in my bag and head to where I am going. How dare it let me down?

'Right in the middle of Knightsbridge. Opposite Harrods of all the places in the world. It had to be there. Acquaintances that I am on nodding terms with walk past me and give me the pity stare, as if I was some homeless person selling *The Big Issue*. I have nowhere else to look, so I wind the windows up and ignore the traffic warden looking at my number plates.

'Is there a problem?' The AA lady repeated. After looking around the car, popping her head in the window, pressing the starter button and giving the dashboard a quick look.

'Obviously, there is a problem. I would not have been sitting here in total humiliation for two hours waiting for someone to come and sort out this damn car.' I vented all my frustration at the so-called mechanic.

'The only problem I can see is that you have run out of petrol, Sir. But not to worry, I have some in my vehicle for these types of incidences. Don't fret, these things happen all the time.' She said in the most patronising voice I have ever heard in my life.'

WHERE DID YOU GET THOSE WORDS? MS SIMONE

340 Word Flash Fiction

'I read it again for the third time, trying to work out where Ms Simone got those words from.'

She must have stared off into the middle distance until her subconscious entered her soul, rummaged around a bit and stirred the imagination, forcing the trickle of words to start entering her mind's eye.

The keyboard intuitively feeling that something new and exciting was afoot, waited in anticipation for the first letter to appear. Her hand's sensing something magical about to happen outstretched themselves. Fingers now relaxed like warriors getting prepared for the next battle, the next victory, slowly pushed themselves, straightening out and then clenched almost as if in a ritual.

And they waited.

Her mind stared patiently into the middle distance, that place where Daoism says perfection lies, until the trickle of interrupted thoughts became a flood and the words came faster than she could type them down.

And still, they came.

Just when she was getting ready for the next verse. It stopped. The thoughts were silent. She suddenly realised that the pool had given all she was going to get for the day.

She tried to force more out; she crinkled her brows, trying to will more words to come, more paragraphs to be shaped, more perfectly formed phrases to come bubbling out into her consciousness.

Nina hoped that the pool would generously give her a poem or a song about the last days of Donald Trump, the ravaging of humanity by COVID, the uncertainties that are covering the world like a depressing blanket. Whether Brexit will push the United Kingdom into more trouble than if we had stayed in Europe, or even if there is anything such as love or is it just needs and wishful desires overruling reality.

But the pool had decided that it would not overfeed Nina. It was only ever going to give her the right amount. Exactly what she needed, not what she wanted.

So, when she came back the next time, it would be replenished and ready to give again.

THE BAD SMELL

200 Word Flash Fiction

---⊗⊗⊗---

He walked into the room from the rose garden. The smell of old socks sneakily avoiding the washing machine because they are suffering from the fear of soap and water, attacked him.

The familiar smell hangs around like an old ashtray or even a mildew-rich concoction, and its voice grows louder as it tries in vain to escape from itself.

Its colour is a dark brown, reminiscent of tar oozing itself away from the cigarette and seeking refuge in a passing lung.

Its pungency reminds him of days running through the dying ash of a forest floor as the embers become laden with the newest downpour of rain and sink further into timeless oblivion.

Energy transposing itself to another plane, another dimension.

The smell hangs there, changing the feel of and the energy

in the room. It made him just want to escape, to smell the fresh air, to find clean oxygen so that his lungs can breathe well once more.

A shapeless entity filled with dark, brooding and ephemeral essence. It comes, it settles, it destroys. Thinks it may roam where ever it wants.

The odour does not know how destructive it is, and frankly, it does not care.

DAMASCUS

200 Word Flash Fiction

I was in the last year of my Master's degree at the best Theology University in our kingdom, and I had even visualised the temple I was going to work in.

I say 'work in', I do not think that teaching the word of God is toil. It is more a calling, a willing contract, where belief overcomes physical evidence and faith reigns.

I had always wanted to become a priest. From the four-year-old thinking, I was the best child of the Lord to the nineteen-year-old knowing, I had a light of inspiration and goodness that I should share with the world.

Our parents, but my mother more so, made sure that each day the faith grew stronger, each month, certainty on anything not tied to my faith flourished less. And in the end, all I had was my faith, my God.

The exam was easy. All the answers just came to me. The

thoughts and ideas were things conceptualised by me a long time ago. Like a professor of religion, I completed the test in no time at all.

Right after they posted the results, I cried in relief. I laughed out loud, in sheer exuberance.

I had failed.

THE LADY IN PRET
A MANGER

150-word flash fiction

———— ⟋⟍ ————

I wrote a message on the Pret A Manger napkin and passed it subtly to the lady sitting in front of me. She picked it up, read it and gazed out the window up to the skyline, challenging the cloud for space.

She turned, looked at me, smiling with her eyes. Lazily, she returned the note saying, 'mind the spelling, mind my time and mind your business, XXX.'

As she flounced out the door, she turned, picked up her half-eaten yoghurt and strolled up Clerkenwell Road as if there she did not have a care in the world. As if life was always going to unfold, stress-free.

I smiled, an enigmatic smile, went back to my hot chocolate drink and almond cake. Mind buzzing from the silent conversation I just had with the lovely lady in the expensive ivory jacket. Her note, 'XXX' and beautiful smile filled me with joy.

ANOTHER TASTE OF MEDIOCRITY

150-word flash fiction

—◦◦◦—

September was a great month for most of the trees in the park.

Their leaves, now tired of hanging around, were dreaming of their long winter holidays in sun-drenched foreign lands with magnolia beaches and deep blue seas.

She trudged wearily up the narrow stairwell to her fourth-floor flat. The bags were so heavy; they were dragging themselves up the stairs and bashing sacks of rice and flour against the concrete steps.

'End of another day,' she thought, heading for the toilet to get rid of that full bladder she had been storing up. All that pain, just to avoid that insect-infested toilet in the park, again.

Bladder sighing with relief, she washed her hands, dried them on the towel she should have changed last week, sat down, exhaled a tired breath and turned the television on.

The highlight of her week, and all the others this year... so far.

SAYING GOODBYE

A 60-word dribble for Mum

It came quietly.

Not a violent, frenetic event, a more calm closing of the eyes as the last breath escaped her tired, stroke-filled frame.

Her face previously enmeshed with memories of each disease, each heart attack, each lung infested infection smoothed out, and the beautiful girl she once was returned.

I noticed all this as I watched my mother die.

ACKNOWLEDGEMENTS

I Would like to thank the editor who worked on this for me to get it error-free. Towards the end of the writing, I could not see a missing comma, full stop or hyphen if it came up and slapped me in the face. Thanks to Charles Phillips for the work he did in helping to turn these ideas from lumps of stones to something I am very proud of.

A great big thank you to my reading group who sat through my readings and gave me insights and inspirational thoughts when I needed them.

ABOUT THE AUTHOR

Roy Merchant was born in Jamaica. He left there in 1961 to join his parents in England. He enlisted in the Royal Navy in 1965 and became a submariner, spending most of his submarine years in Singapore, Hong Kong, and other parts of the Far East.

Having left the Navy in 1970, he retrained as an Electronics Engineer, then Technical Manager in a large television rental company in the 1970s.

In the mid-'80s, he moved into local government as a senior manager in a London local authority. Retiring in 2014, Roy took a fresh path and started a Health and well-being company catering for the African Caribbean community while dedicating more time to writing and performing poetry across London.

This book is his fourth, his third is a novella called *Distorted Lens*, his second is *20 Things I Wish I Knew At 20*, and *Walking In The Shadows Of Death* was his first.

Published by:

Relentless Realities
Roy Merchant   Writer and Performance Poet
Website: https://www.relentless-realities.com
Email: roy@relentless-realities.com

www.ingramcontent.com/pod-product-compliance
Lightning Source LLC
Chambersburg PA
CBHW021120130626
46554CB00002B/790